A FIGHT FOR A

DREAM

TEM APROPHIS EMILE

TABLE OF CONTENTS

ACKNOWLEDGEMENTS

◆ ◆ ◆

I am grateful to God Almighty for giving me the strength, courage, energy and inspiration to write. It was journey of self-discovery that allowed me to reflect deeply. I learnt more about myself and my love for writing.

I would also like to thank my entire family for their continuous help, support and love. To all my friends and colleagues at Alfa Education Douala; I say thank you for all your love, charity and friendship.

I am also grateful to IGWE Jonathan for believing in me.

To my mentors Kimberly Burnham and Snehal Singh (Mind Spirit Works), I say thanks for igniting an eternal writing flame.

CHAPTER ONE:
THE BIRTHDAY PARTY

◆ ◆ ◆

"**M**y name is TEM Dany. I am seven years old, a boy, the third child in a family of four. My seventh birthday marked the beginning of the end of faint joy that existed in my family. Civil war was upon us and we were severely hit by hardship and poverty. The streets were now occupied by flies and insects which feasted on the numerous corpses scattered all across the streets. Schools and daily activities came to a halt and the daily hustle and bustle in large cities had all died down. The only sound left on the morbidly quiet streets of the cities were the sounds of bullets gushing through the air. It had been two years since the war. One day I remembered my father telling us that things will soon come back to normal because the white people were putting their heads together to resolve matters.

This was a rare day when the whole family laughed as my younger brother had asked "Does it mean they will remain without heads since they are putting their heads together?" This laughter lasted a short while after which my father explained to us what he meant. I could see my father's weakened strength through his eyes. A false sense of security that failed time and time again. He was afraid. We knew that.

The rebels had gained grounds and things had become worse as people were forced to remain indoors. The hospitals were littered with wounded soldiers everywhere. Every day, my parents had to go to a camp and meet a long line of people waiting for food from the N.G.O as he called them. This was the only means by which most families could get food. We lost our younger brother, who was only three years old at the time to Malaria which had gain grounds in the country due to the accumulations of filth.

I remember sitting at a corner of the room and covered my ears with the pillow not to hear the sorrowful choruses sung by my mother and the crying and lamentations of my sister. My parents were more worried about her than myself. They always did.

My elder brother was always silent and looked at the events of life with such bitterness. He was angry with the misery we were living in and was sad because he was helpless. I remember him saying to our parents in tears after we had gone several days without eating "Mother, father, I promise you that when I become a man, I will provide you with all your needs, even if it's the last thing I will do. I promise you, we shall be happy one day". That was the only day I saw him crying. He didn't even when our younger brother passed away.

My brother was a strange person. He loved arranging wooden swords and playing games of death. We were his only friends. Most of the times, my sister and I would play the role of the captives and him our hero. I enjoyed the gymnastics he did with his sword and the brave words he pronounced when he came to free us. He developed this passion from the movie "Gladiator" which was my father's favourite.

One day when we were all sat for dinner, my father announced that he was thinking of celebrating my seventh birthday. The news left us all feeling indifferent and no one even budged from their seats. My mother had her hands on her cheek and looked at him in pity. I thought it was a joke because even I had forgotten the day I was born and I knew he had no money to organise such a thing. He went on persuading everyone and said "where there is a will, there is a way." There were five days to go to my birthday and the chaos that had reigned in our minds had disappeared. Not even the sounds of guns disturbed us. The fighting in the streets had intensified. The prolonged hunger and thirst in the country let to highway armed robbery and kidnapping. Most youth had indulged into criminal activities and drug trafficking to survive. Houses were attacked and burnt. The singing of birds and melodies of nature were replaced by crying and screaming of terrorised children and women. None of the events above disturbed the small amount of merriment that we had in our hearts.

At the eve of my birthday, my father brought out news papers from his cupboard to be refashioned as decoration. This was a hidden talent my mother had. She could take any old and dilapidated object and renew it into a beauty of decoration. Leaves of different colours were used and our parlour was transformed. For a short period, the pain, suffering and sorrow was forgotten.

The day of my birthday had finally arrived and our parlour was lively. Nothing special was done, but just to have the feeling of being alive and united was enough. My family sat close to me and we held our hands and prayed. I heard my mother asking God to tilt the minds of mankind and humanity towards the virtues of love and righteousness. Her last words to God before every one gave an "Amen" were for Him to protect and save our family and our country at large.

Many questions started going through my mind concerning the whereabouts of God and the power God had on humanity. I questioned Him. What kept Him so long and why He was silent about the derailment of mankind. My deep thoughts were interrupted by the singing of my birthday song. It was the same song my mother sang to me when I was breast fed. They said it was my sleeping pill. For the first time I saw numerous smiles on the faces of my family members and the hope for a better tomorrow was rekindled, but for how long? We ate the little food that was prepared and started reflecting on our past days and glory.

The night had been long and everyone exhausted. Before we could finish assembling everything to catch our cold tender bed, we heard a thunderous noise on the door and the frail nails, flew up in the air as a skydiver. Before we realised what was going on, a group of armed men dashed in and started harassing everyone in the house.

They said nothing and bundled my mother and sister. My father on his honour could not watch this happen. He tried to intervene, but was knocked down by one of the men with his wicket gun. How I wished I was blind not to see such a scene. All the elements of my body were attacked by fear and I was trembling, feeling as a fragile leaf. My eyes caught those of my brother and you can imagine how he felt.

My mother and sister were carried out of the house and their endless screaming provoked my father. He tried to get up and I heard the sound of a gunshot! IT was a menacing and vile sound! It was the first time I heard that sound. I remember bringing my knees close to my chest as I sat down in a corner and closed my eyes.

As I opened my eyes, I saw my father lying in own his blood. My brother burst out and dived on one of the men, but the same fate befell him. All these scenes unfolded in the eyes of a seven-year-old. I felt my heart wasn't taking in air any longer. I remember forcing myself to catch what little air left in the parlour and the continuous weeping and shouting of my mother and sister which echoed deep into my ears. I blacked out.

CHAPTER TWO:
A CAMP ON FIRE

◆ ◆ ◆

I was awakened the next morning by our neighbours who heard the entire scene. They gave me some drugs because I was still trembling with uncontrollable fear. They buried the corpses. My mother and sister were nowhere to be found. I was certain that they were sold as slaves to a neighbouring country or to the rebels. I sat for several hours alone in the parlour lamenting and the traumatising images came over and over in my mind. I left the house to run away from these images, asking myself what I'd do next. A neighbour could shelter me for a while but not for ever. After deliberation. they all decided to take me to a refugee camp where I could be fed and sheltered.

The camp was a disgusting and nasty place. It was built by a Non-Government Organization (N.G.O) in a bid to prevent homeless people from facing danger. The population there could not be contained by the camp, and this resulted in shortages.

I had no choice but to embrace the life in the camp. I joined the local camp school and sat with children of my age. The only difference was that they were with their parents while I was alone. I had not gone to school for the last two years. I did not like the idea but had no choice. I sat there speechless looking at the teacher and wondering what he was expecting from me. The other children were scared of me because I never talked to anyone and never smiled. I was always absent-minded and everyone became worried. The families in the camp drove me away when I came near them.

Every Sunday I joined the others in church. I found myself spending all my time in church because no one chased me out of there. Every day I saw people coming with their problems to present them before someone they could not see. All of them felt different after they had finished talking to Him. "Did He give them what they asked? Can He bring back my family? But how can one person listen and solve the problems of all these people here? "I think my own problems are too difficult", I said to myself before falling asleep on one of the chairs.

The following weeks at camp were more difficult than previously due to the influx of a water borne disease. A good number of people were affected by this disease and most of them died. Gatherings were discouraged and children stopped going to school. Some people ran away from the camp. They preferred to face guns in the cities than seeing their destinies decided upon by cholera. I was lucky to avoid being infected by cholera, because I ate little and did not associate with people. Cries of sorrows and weeping had over taken the habitual songs and choirs in the camp. The cousin of death had installed its head quarters in the camp. A counter offensive was launched by people of good will and measures were taken to combat cholera. Health specialists were sent and the camp was freed of this epidemic.

Games and competitions were organised in the camp to alleviate the sorrows in peoples face. I sat in a distant seat and no one noticed me, as usual. I watched the other children buried in excitement as they won the numerous prizes.

I wondered why happiness was that discriminatory. All my life, it had never come my way. We only met on particular occasions organised by my parents who could hear the words from my silence. As I looked at the other children, I was even more convinced that my place was not in a camp. I remembered the advice my father gave us, that a real man when grown up must get married and have children which must be followed by taking care of and protecting them. I however knew that to chase, these goals while staying in the camp, was like chasing the wind.

Years went by and I was now ten. The situation in the country was gradually improving but still unstable since the rebels had embarked on suicide bombing. One gentle morning, two innocent female faces between 12 and 14 entered the camp. Their dresses were torn and twisted. Their lips were cracked and dry as a desert. Their pitiful faces made everyone feel sympathy for them. The nurses ran and took them along for a consultation. Everyone was on his habitual daily activities till a thunderous sound was heard. These sound made the ground tremble with all the people around. There was an ecstasy of panic in everyone's mind then we saw the dispensary on fire. All the men in the camp ran toward it to save what could be saved. As it was built with tents, the flame smiled on it and went wild. Men started resisting it so as not to have it consume the whole camp.

At that moment no one thought of those that were in the dispensary or the origin of the fire. The fire was defeated but several people perished including the nurses. Fire expert came and traces of explosives were found at the scene. It was concluded that those two strangers were suicide bombers and that the same fate had been felt in other camps. People sad with their hands folded, others with hands on their cheek. "What are they thinking or looking at?" I asked to myself. I'm sure they were seeing the two nurses that had been so lovely and kind to them and nature, being carried up by the wind. All I knew was that I had to leave this place.

Days passed and I assessed my three years in the camp and was tired of the circle that it formed, because I did the same things every day and went to the same places. I was determined to put an end to this. I had erased the day of my birth day on all the calendars I came by. To me it was on this same day that I was brought to this wicked world and on this same day my family was shattered. These were enough reasons for me never to forgive this day. My craving for escape was growing day by day. I stared preparing my way out. Since my movement from school to church had improved my reading skills, I constantly read the bible but was still sceptical of its teaching. My determination made me have a bad reputation in the camp since I gave in to the theft of people's money and valuable objects. Each time I did it, I had an internal judge questioning me. This made me sometimes feel uncomfortable because I had to justify myself with what life itself had done to me.

I would ask if it was God who was interrogating me, and then burst out, still in my thought with a frown in my face saying "where were you when my family was destroyed, and why don't you bring back my mother and sister. Just leave me alone."

With these words I continued with my acts until I thought what I had was enough for me to face the streets. One night, I left the camp in search for my mother and sister.

CHAPTER THREE:
THE CAR ACCIDENT

◆ ◆ ◆

I entered the town. My destination was my father's house. The streets were as empty as a robbed room. The only things that could be seen were empty houses and abandoned cars. Some buildings had new designs from what their owners gave them. Certainly, it was the new look bullets and bombs had given them. The town seemed like a ghost city. I knew the way to our house and hurried there.

When I saw what was left of our house, I was filled with grief. All our neighbors were nowhere to be found. As I went in tears filled my eyes. In less than a minute, my t-shirt was soaked. I sat on the dusty chair and saw the plate my father was eating on, that pathetic night. The plate was in a pitiful state from the numerous aggressions it had suffered from the elements of nature. I was over taken by a flashback in which I remembered my father telling us that, this house was his lifetime dream. My father told us how it took him sleepless night and restless days to put it up and was ready to scale the tops of Mount Fako to realize his dreams.

This flash back made me doubt whether my Father had been happy after achieving his goal. I was not certain with my answer to this question; this was because I thought of all the hardship we had gone through. We had been living at the mercy of the wind, which was generally stormy on us and gentle on others around us. The only brief moments of happiness were when our father sold some flowers he nursed back to health, since he was a gardener. The sales were made by God's grace. My father had a passion for environmental beauty. He was fond of speaking to flowers and treated them in such a special way. He always went out of control when he saw people mistreating plants. He had hoped his children had the same passion as him but left us to choose our destinies.

I was fixated on the idea that happiness was tribalistic and discriminatory. Moving to all the corners of the fallen dreams of his father, I vowed to myself to chase happiness where ever it was. Thus, I thought it wise to work hard and acquire wealth. I would be happy and my father where ever he was, will also be happy seeing me happy.

I spent the night there. As I opened the bible which I took with me, I came through on a passage denouncing theft and waywardness. I was reluctant to proceed with my reading. I said in a guilty voice "ok, fine, I will not steal again if you bring back my mother and sister".

Without knowing, I had started developing a personal relationship with the Almighty. I wanted to see manifest, his powers on my life, because up till then, I had seen nothing. The night in the town was not as peaceful as in the camp. Every corner of the house seemed colder and more frightful. Only the sounds made by its new occupants in their hide out were heard. In my mind, the fear of being killed meant nothing to me because I had thought of death as an option to escape all this suffering. This option had crossed my mind on several occasions but an internal voice had always discouraged me. I had a dream that night and in it, they were blaming me for not intervening to defend my family. I did not recognise the faces of my prosecutors.

In my dream, they took me in a camp were children soldiers were being trained and armed to go and cause sorrows to mankind. People were bundled and we were asked to open fire on them. I woke up from my dream screaming with all my strength 'mamaaa!'. I was trembling with a strange fear because I saw my mother amongst the people that were being bundled.

I only regained my composure when I realised that it was a dream. I was weakened by this dream but had to move forward. My goal was to chase happiness at all cost.

Early in the morning, I went to the yard at the back of the house where my family were buried. I did not recognise the real spot because everywhere was bushy. I kneeled and asked my father to guide me and give me strength to face the streets and realise my dreams. I left and began my journey.

I slept in abandoned cars and houses. I came in contact with other street boys and made friends with them. As the youngest in the group, I generally obeyed older mates. We spend most of our times in markets and public places. I became a professional pick pocket. We left our victims perplexed and speechless when they were about to get into their transaction. Sometimes our coups went unsuccessful and the hunter became the hunted. Those caught were given a snake beating. These made some of us so scared that they had to abandon their flocks. I had gone deep in this new way of life that I started smoking as others. I was the luckiest fellow among us, because of my innocent face, I had never been caught. My friends mocked me when they saw me with a Bible, they referred to me as 'saint rat' meaning the "holy thief". I was not happy with this nickname but could do nothing. I knew I was shying away from the Holy path and did not want to be reminded of it.

The security men had already taken note of us and we were been chased everywhere we were seen. Life had become complicated for us and our numbers drastically reduced. We spent most of our time hiding in our holes. After weeks of hunger, we went back to our job and fell into an ambush set by the police.

I was at the front line and found myself face to face with the police. "Oh God, I am finished!" I cried. Millions of thoughts ran through my mind. I thought of what, I had heard about prison, the promise I made to myself and instantly I concluded, 'Prison…Never!' At the speed of lightening, I flew between two of the police men. They only realised what had happened when I was already several steps away from them and they jumped behind me. My senses were dominated by a strange fear and this made my reasoning dormant. I dashed into the road without looking and was knocked down by a car. Every one ran closer to have a look at my situation.

My friends used these opportunity and disappeared. Each of them was taking his own direction, meaning that was the end of our group. Those that were close to me shaded tears as they thought I was death. The policemen carried me to the hospital and left me under the care of a health specialist.

CHAPTER FOUR:
CLEANING UP THE NEW DREAM

◆ ◆ ◆

I was unconscious and was taken to the emergency ward. I was registered under social welfare which was to take care of me after treatment. A few hours after a specialist had worked on me, I regained consciousness but was still feeble. I saw men and women in white moving endlessly. They all seamed pre-occupied and talked in a slow tune. One of them came to me. She looked sleepy, tired and exhausted. She smiled at me and looked at my eyes then the tubes attached to my body. Before leaving, she said something which I did not hear.

Minute by minute beds were emptied and new occupants admitted. I saw all sorts of traumatizing cases. I saw people badly injured and others suffering and weakened by pains.

Every fifteen minutes the calmness was interrupted by screaming of sorrows which were echoed repeatedly from the walls. These were the worst days in my life. I started regretting all the wrong things I had engaged in which brought me here. Every time the people in white came, I wished they were coming to discharge me. I started thinking of God but was afraid because I had gone against him. I however acknowledged the fact that my life was far better than that of those I saw at the emergency.

The whole night I tried to understand the relationship between life, nature and God. But every theory I built was inexact because each person had an individual life and reality. I then resolved to take everything the way it came without questioning. All this was to be guided by the commandments of the creator.

I now had the conviction that God had loved and protected me ever since. I was told by a nurse to wait for the social welfare personnel who were to take charge of me. I knew I was going directly to prison. With a shy look, I pointed at the nurse and asked with my head down "What will happen to me there?" The nurse smiled at me and said "don't worry, they'll take good care of you there."

"Where are your parents?" she asked. Tears filled my eyes after her question. I opened my month but the voice did not come out. The nurse did not understand what was wrong but comforted me and said, "At the orphanage, you'll make new friend and you'll have a new family."

These last words were too biter for my ears. I said to myself that I'll rather die than having a new family. I asked to go the toilet and was directed to one. I managed to leave without anyone's attention. I found myself back in the street and decided to create a job for myself. I went to a nearby market and started picking up papers and trash everywhere in order to keep the place clean. I weeded the low grass with my hands and some people threw me some coins as they passed. Others congratulated me. As I sat sadly, some sympathizing souls gave me food and water. I did not stay there for long because I was driven away by a committee that kept the market clean. To them I was gaining peoples sympathy thereby reducing their weekly income.

I thought of going to clean hospitals but my past experience with hospitals made me vow never to go near one again. I made my way to parks and first thought of loading and off loading luggage in cars but this needed strength. I continued with the picking of papers and washing of cars. With the little money I had, I bought a broom, bucket and rags. I swept places without asking anyone. Some welcomed me while others rebuked and chased me away.

Some car owners who had been victims of unscrupulous people gave me a hard time when they saw me wiping their cars without their permission. I was almost taken to the police by a woman who mistook me for someone else. Luckily, she let me off. Just the thought of going to the police made me panic. Quickly, I took my belongings and started wandering helplessly to nowhere in particular. I saw my entire future wrapped up inside a bag. I sat on a public chair and saw thousand of hopeless people suffering the ravages of the war. The emptiness I saw in their faces made me more determined not to end up like them.

My greatest problem now was finding a place to sleep. I used the rags as my pillow and lay looking at the stars. I remembered a conversation with my elder brother in which he told me he had always believed that the stars represent the good people who had gone to heaven. I looked at the multitude of stars, asking which of them represented my family members. I worriedly asked myself, "Why must we die before going up there? All those who love war and killing should be left down here and peaceful people should be brought up there". My beautiful imagination was intercepted by a sudden sleep from a stressful day.

I was awakened by the numerous sounds of cars like the chorus of weevils in the bush. My eyes opened, I realised I was on the ground. I did not even remember when I nodded off. My heart jumped when I realised my working materials had disappeared. Only the rag on the chair was spared. Certainly the night hunters had passed by. I was perplexed at the level of determination of these people. I asked to myself "Even brooms and bucket?!" Furiously, I burst out of my silence and shouted to the hearing of all in the street "cowards, it's only on me that you can exercise your courage and determination, fools." As I spoke alone in a loud voice, the passers-by turned toward me with their unconcerned looks, each in their busy steps, they stared at me like one of the mentally derailed.

To me, this was the drop that over flowed the stream. I could not bear this suffering anymore. Bitter tears started flowing down my eyes and my anger transformed to melancholy. In a low sorrowful tune, I said "What type of life is this? What have I done badly to this world? Papa, mama where are you? Please come and take me to where you are." I sat for a long time beaten down by my thought and knew crying will not solve my problems. I wiped my tears, took my rag and left. I walked hungrily in the streets and entered a railway station. I saw dusty chairs and rubbish hanging in various spots. Without any permission I went and picked up all the trash and assembled them in a nylon, then to the trash can. With my rag I started dusting all the chairs. Before I could finish, an angry voice came from behind demanding me to stop. I turned and saw an old angry face coming towards me. He was dressed like a school boy. On his shirt was written "security."

"Young man what are you doing, and who are you?" he asked bitterly. Little did I know that such acts were suspicious due to the insecurity in the country.

Travellers had certainly been victims of vandalism. The furiousness on his face almost knocked me down. My face was in its most pitiful and innocent appearance. The old worn out face was staring at me in terror waiting for the response to his questions. "I am Dany and I am looking for a job to have something to eat, please help me." I said.

These words healed the broke and flaring temper of the old man. He had never been this touched in his entire life. He looked at the pale child in front of him and the only words he said next were 'my child come with me'. He presented himself as Uncle Sam and took me to a room where he was living behind the park. He gave me the little food he had and I felt on it like a hungry lion with no mercy.

Uncle Sam was almost in tears when he saw an innocent boy almost fighting with the bowl. I took a large sip of water and a deep breath and looked to Uncle Sam as my saviour.

CHAPTER FIVE:
THE JOURNEY FOR A BETTER TOMORROW

———————

◆ ◆ ◆

After I had taken some time to digest the food, Uncle Sam was back from his duty post and had come to counsel me. I narrated in tears all the tribulation I had gone through until then. Uncle Sam played the silent listener; he was truly astonished and did not know what to say. He looked at me and asked me to stop crying. "It is good you have decided to pursue happiness my son, because there is no happiness without money and here there is no money." Uncle Sam told me I could stay with him and assist in doing the cleaning but I should climb all mountains if necessary, not to end up as him.

Early the next morning, Uncle Sam took me to all the places he had to clean. He presented me to the personnel of the park and immediately I began work. I did the cleaning with such passion that I won the favours of the park users. Uncle Sam showed me love and attention and in return I made the old man always happy with my work. The old man often narrated to me events of his childhood and the dreams he had. His greatest dream was to become a professor, so as to have an impact on the lives of many youths. He went on saying "my child, forever in life knowledge will govern ignorance, that is, an uneducated child is like a timed bomb to his country. The easy recruitment of child soldier is the result of the level of illiteracy which has as companion, poverty and misery. But if an uneducated person is willing to succeed, then he should be prepared to work double and even triple compared to an educated person."

I, knowing my thoughts about school, started having doubts as to what I was chasing. I asked my friend "Is happiness meant for some people and not for others?" Uncle Sam looked at my worried face and said, "Happiness is for everyone, but we have to go for it the right way. Let me assure you, you will never find happiness in this country because here dreams end up only as dreams they never transform to reality."

I grew pale when I heard that. I thought of all the dreams my family had. What about the dreams of these people moving all around the cities? The old man realised that I had become absent-minded. He thought it wise to train my mind with the reality of things for me to be better prepared.

"Never be desperate my son. God is still alive. Just go on and keep nourishing, watering and building your dreams. They might one day turn to reality".

I looked at him and all I asked was to be given a bible.

The following days, we went on with our day to day activities. I had more interest and desire to go overseas. I did the cleaning so well that I was motivated by all. I gave this money to my friend to keep. During my spare time I read the Bible to strengthen my relationship with God. On several occasions I dreamt of my mother and sister. I asked them to follow the sun as the Magi kings followed the moon and stars according to the Bible story, and you shall also find me.

Uncle Sam introduced me to a group of young men who were all planning the overseas journey. Preparations were made and everyone was ready for the D-day. The old man added his saving to mine. I assured the old man to return if things turned out better.

On D-day, we left for the pursue of happiness. I and my new peers embarked on a long and unfamiliar journey. Everything went smoothly since we had money. We got to the North of Africa. I started falling short of money, due to the various check points we had to settle. We were dropped far off from town since we had no legal papers. The poor people living at the peripherals were less concerned with our presence since the battle for survival was more important. I saw thousands of oversee seekers like me. All were blocked by a vast imposing force of nature. I heard people calling it the Mediterranean Sea. The new comers that we were, saw other people who had been there for years and each recounted how they had seen the face of death, but God's hand brought them back.

The unfortunate ones were of blessed memories. Just by looking at these people, my dreams started fading away. I became certain that the problems in my country were an African problem in general. I was certainly impressed by the solidarity of the blacks living there but knew that the success of each will depend on his individual actions and efforts.

Days went by and my life started moving backward. Everyone was preoccupied with what life was reserving for him. I moved all-round the neighbourhood and saw people harbouring sad sitting postures. They were all seeing their dreams carried away by the sea. Just as the sea, the police hindered people from entering into the town to look for jobs. The traumatising hunger forced desperate souls to work for drug dealers and human traffickers to have something to eat. The young girls were taken to town and used as prostitutes while the boys supplied drugs all over the town. The rise of these criminal acts in town made life difficult at the peripherals. This was due to the rampant police raids. Those who were caught were either imprisoned or repatriated. Some jumped into the sea to avoid being caught. I and others were lucky as we found refuge in a nearby bush. I sat on the shore watching the sea. I had been for days without sleeping normally. I started regretting my country and the decision I took to come here. Holding my bible in my hand, I taught of Moses and the Red Sea. How I hoped the same faith could take place in that instant. I stretched my hands at the Sea several times but nothing happened. Those seated on the other side looked at me and laughed saying hunger had made me brave.

In the next few hours, I decided to join a group of youths who were to enter the town. We had to choose, between facing the security men and dying of hunger. We crossed the red line in our numbers with unprecedented speed. The outnumbered security men fired those they could, but the others crossed running into the town. Once in town we took different directions.

My eyes saw the beauty of construction. Every place was fashioned and designed in such a special way that my hungry stomach was satisfied. I had never seen such a wonderful environment. The people on the streets were disciplined and conservative in their lifestyle. I was however disappointed because I could not proceed with my job since everywhere was clean. I was moving in the street as a ghost. It seemed all the eyes of the people stared at me.

I became scared, looking for somewhere to hide but did not see any. It was clear that the numerous eyes on me were telling me I was not one of them. I moved to a nearby park and watched the children there playing, singing and recounting tales with their friends and I became furious with life and started thinking negative. I ate the left over from a nearby trash can and the endless patrols of the police almost gave me a heart attack. I hid myself up a tree till it was dark.

The gentle breeze blowing up the tree reminded me of my father and a peaceful mornings when he trained us on how to plant trees. I remembered him saying "Women are just as these flowers. You'll never see their true beauty if you don't take good care of them. Look at how beautiful your mother is. It's only when I learned to take care of flowers that I understood how to deal with her. Look at her eyes, aren't they more beautiful than the morning stars." We all turned looking at our mother with a smile. I waved my hands at her. Like a shy bird she smiled back at us going to the other end not to hear other praises of her.

These sweet memories almost made me fall out of the tree as I had forgotten myself. I managed to hold tight to a branch and remained up. I had a good view of the town and saw two boys over the road entering a building. I knew I needed somewhere to sleep. I came down the tree and went to that building. I took courage and went in. The faces I saw almost made me take my fastest speed out of the building. I was approached by one who asked "who are you and what do you want." My heart leaped, my trembling legs almost brought me down. I looked left and right and saw other boys waiting and confident in themselves. I replied with my head down, "I have nowhere to go and nowhere to sleep, please keep me here, I am ready to work."

The men were drug dealers and were looking for boys like me to distribute their goods. I was immediately given a place to sleep while the other boys went on a last commission. I was drilled on what to do and the next day I was to start supplying drugs to customers.

CHAPTER SIX:
THE POLICE RAID

◆ ◆ ◆

I had a sleep so deep that night that I did not hear all the movements and noise. I was suddenly kicked by an angry foot accompanied by a cruel voice which urged me to get up before he passed me. I got up almost walking on four legs and joined the other boys. They took me onto a field and I asked if that was all we had to do. I went back to work and within a short while, I had started saving money. I went with a sachet of drugs to the client and came back with money for my boss. I was given commissions for each transactions.

Unfortunately, as time went by, most of the boys with whom I was working with had been arrested and some killed by the dealers. Most confrontations between the dealers always ended with several killings. I often found myself in the middle of trouble. Neither the police nor the relentless dealers were to spare us. Most of the dealers we were working with had fled the country. We started living a hide and seek life.

One hot afternoon, two boys approached me. I saw smiles passing over the face of one of the boys and I wondered what could be the cause. Had the authorities decided to help us or was there a ship waiting for us? All these questions went through my mind before the boys unveiled why they had come. The said that they had been contacted by a group of men that needed young volunteers to work with them. I did vow never do anything illegal but I decided to hear what they had to say.

I was taken to a place and noticed Arab writings all over the walls. The other boys needed me by them because I was the only one amongst them who could read and write. At times, I read the bible to them and they looked amazed. When I was with them, I realised the importance of being educated. This made me feel superior to them. Two men came and we were taken in a hall. Instantly, I became overwhelmed with Islamic propagandas everywhere just as I used to see on television. "Oh father, I am dead." I exclaimed in a low voice. The other boys started panicking as they heard me. One of them asked worriedly "Why? What is the problem?" They saw a strange fear in me.

I vividly had memories of all the suicide bombings and havoc they had caused. Immediately, I told them "let's get out of here at once!" "You are scarfing me. What is wrong?" asked one of my friends. The other boy angrily burst out "What is wrong with you people?! These men are ready to pay us a huge sum of money. I can't remain this poor. Whatever they ask us to do I will do!"

I looked at the ignorant boy and asked "Do you know what they do for a living? Are you ready to serve as a human bomb or will you kill people just to get rich?" These questions almost stopped air from getting into their lungs. They looked at each other and were speechless.

One of the men came to us with food and drinks. We had lost appetite. The hunger in us had disappeared. I started eating to avoid any suspicion and the others joined me. The man smiled and said to us, "After eating I will take you to a man who will train you on what to do." Immediately after the man left, we looked for a way out. When we saw the door leading outside the hall, the three of us had the same thought. WE RAN! We continued running with no particular direction. We escaped.

We sat to rest in a yard of a school. Watching other children living a normal childhood life. One of the boys asked "What did we do to deserve this? Are you sure God is still alive?" I was silent for a while and replied "Certainly He is still alive and am sure He will one day shower His mercy on us." With this, I had become their leader and their source of hope. Their level of illiteracy was higher than mine.

We went to one of the client of our former boss who was also a dealer, he gave us accommodation and we started supplying for him. Things were flourishing and I got in contact with a 'boatman.' They were those who transported people illegally to Europe in their ships. I got all the information on the day they were to leave. I became aggravated when they told me the amount of money I had to pay. I knew I could never afford that amount of money. The idea of returning back to my country became more apparent than ever.

Two days before the ship was to leave for Italy, I met a client. The client I met had a hard time. He had kept me waiting for hours. The other boys were through with their commissions and had returned to our headquarters. The client finally came and handed me the money for the transaction and I finally left. My boss and my friends had become worried because of my delay. Then, they heard a knock at the door. My boss was preparing to batter me if I had no explanation for delaying his money.

As the doorbell rang, everyone knew I was the one returning from my errand. Unfortunately for them, it was a police raid. The was total panic in the hall as the police men pointed guns at every direction. Everyone was asked to embrace the floor. The po-po were all dressed in black and their faces veiled. Their bodies were fortified with ammunition. One of the boys out of panic, urinated on his dress and in a sulky voice he cried endlessly "mama, mama, please come and help me, come and take me home"

I was a few metres away from our headquarters when I saw irregular movement out of the house. Immediately I saw policemen coming outside of the house with its occupant arrested. Without hesitating, I took an about turn and was almost knocked down by a car as I crossed the road without looking. I ran the whole night on the empty streets crying for I knew that was all about my friends.

I got tired and stopped to rest. I almost forgot that I had a huge sum of money with me. I was wondering what will happen to my friends. Suddenly, I thought of the 'passeur'. I took my way to the dock. I met those in charged and proposed to be harboured for the remaining days in a ship then transported to Italy. Before the 'passure' could offer a word, I passed the huge sum of money for the services I needed.

The money was more than enough. The man had no choice than to accept the deal. I knew that without the money the man will not have any empathy towards me. Soon after, the man began treating me like a prince and he even was explaining how life was in Europe. I began to realise how powerful money was and I became more determined to go for it.

CHAPTER SEVEN:
THE SEA OF A MILLION SORROWS

◆ ◆ ◆

I was feeling blue and down for days. The ship was full beyond capacity. I looked at the faces of both the old and young; leaving behind the pain and sorrow, wanting to find a better tomorrow. I looked at a woman seated at one end breastfeeding her baby. She did all she could for the baby. The men around her pushed and fell on her without sympathy. All she cared about was her baby. I felt pity for her and realized what my father always said to us "mother is great." I asked to myself what was wrong with Africa, was it Africa that was poor or was it Africans who had a poor mental outlook.

Despite all the sorrows caused by the sea of a million sorrows, the Africans still confronted it. All of us saw it as our last chance of hope. However, the calmness that came out of it was more frightful than hell. The voices of those buried beneath it were heard by the silent passers-by. I became scared and immediately embarked on saying my prayers. We were travelling for several days and yet, no sight of land could be seen.

The weather worsened as heavy storms began pouring continuously. These awoke the sea from its slumber. The sea started behaving like a wild beast and the ship began moving violently. The whole crew knew it was their last hope as they cried out; unanimous shouting and screaming.

I sat holding my arms closely to my knees; praying, "Oh father, so this is the end, the end of a pathetic and disgusting life. Father please ….!"

Before I knew it, people tumbling on me, and under the water everybody went.

I fell into a deep coma and my soul was in heaven with my family. I was happy to see my parents and fell in their arms. I told my mother I wanted to eat that delicious corn fufu and bitter leaf she used to cook when I was still a kid. "Oh I almost forgot, please take me to God, I have to see Him and thank Him for protecting me when I was down there. How does He look? Is He too old? Please bring me to Him."

I heard people murmuring around me and their gentle voices made it clear to me that I was with angels. I opened my eyes timidly and asked "Am I really in heaven?" A nurse came closer to me and said "Not yet my boy, you are in a hospital, everything will be alright." I looked around and saw hundreds of people in the same condition as I and asked "What happened?" The nurse narrated to me how we were saved by the coastguard from almost drowning.

I was in tears. The realisation of being alive and far from my family in heaven made me almost grow mad. Not even the fact that I was in Italy, the very same Italy that I had been dreaming of for this while. The nurse empathised with me. She understood the pain and suffering. She almost felt it. She reassured me saying, "Don`t cry boy, we are going to take care of you." The other survivors and I were cared for with such humility and love, and this accelerated our recovery.

I was moved by the attitudes of the whites who came to us. They were calm and lovely. They provided us with food and clothing. Their words were soft and tender. From their eyes one could see sincerity. I realized I had gone a million steps forward towards realizing my dreams. Here, human beings were given an impetus for being alive, compared to what was taking place in some African countries. I was back on my feet and taken to a refugee camp with the others.

I still had a negative memory of camp life and despite the numerous facilities there, I was a camp hater. I was certain that if I went all around the city and did my cleaning campaigns then I would earn some money. All I needed were my working tools and all will be fine. My greatest fear was, if I were caught and repatriated, all my efforts and sufferings would have been useless.

After several months in the camp, I started monitoring the movement of the security men. I had to take the risk and enter the city rather than living the monitored life in the camp.

One day, I fell ill and was admitted in the hospital. There, I met some boys who had the same plan as me and we fraternised with one another. The next day, we were out of the camp. We took different directions and my heart started racing faster as I entered the town. I was taken aback by the beauty of the city. I walked and looked at the signs on the streets but the writings were unfamiliar to me. "This is more beautiful than my la-la land," I said to myself.

Before I realized it, I walking for hours and did not see a single place that needed cleaning. Since every place seemed new and well looked after. I thought of hospitals and headed for one but then stopped and changed my direction as I saw security men at the entrance. All the parks I went to were cleaner than many homes in my country. I went into a park and started cleaning the floor. I said to myself all I needed was for them to thank me and maybe I might touch a soft chord in their hearts. To my greatest surprise two men started running towards me. The two men had the same attire and they were pointing at me dangerously. "Certainly this is not an friendly run," I said to myself as I dropped everything and ran for my dear life.

Saved from danger, my mind grew troubled. I started having second thoughts about my host country. "What is wrong with these people? Is this how they treat us in their country? No one looks at you peacefully, no one addresses you. How am I going to survive here? Where will I find happiness if I can`t even smile? Is it because I learned nothing in school, or because I came here illegally? Lord, you are my last and only hope in this confusing world."

CHAPTER EIGHT:
DANY'S ARREST

◆ ◆ ◆

I soon realised how important education was overseas. I started loitering around school compounds watching other children living a care free life, smiling over their future. One day I was noticed by a teacher. She came to me and asked who I was and what I was looking for. I took a deep breath and presented myself. I pleaded to her, asking for permission to study; get into her school. She that only the school director could admit me. She concluded that I should stop hanging around the school premises for security purposes.

I left the gate and was determined to talk to the director. I kept on wandering around the premises noting the time of arrival and departure of staff. I equally noticed a certain black car that always came last and was packed at the same spot every day. The person driving the car always came out first and opened the door for the person sitting behind. I was not wrong with my conclusion that such a person should be the director of the school. I waved at the car every time the car was entering and going out of the school but it never stopped.

I did not relent my efforts. I was determined to follow the director right to his house to tell him my problems. Each time the car came out of the school, I ran behind it but always got tired and lost on the way. The next day I sat where I lost sight of them and continued chasing from there as they passed by. The driver had noticed me and he changed his direction. I went for days without seeing them passing. The next morning, I headed to the school and stood opposite the road until I saw the car entering. I made my little prayer and dashed inside the gate. Some school pupils hanging around stared at me. It seemed they were scared of me. I walked timidly to the path leading to the main door, "Who are you and where are you going?!" a voice stopped me from behind. I turned my trembling legs towards the voice. From her attire, she looked like one of the school personnel. Her voice was heavier than her size. Her face was twisted as she came closer to me. She was tall. Before I could utter a word, she asked me to leave before she called the police. Just the name police made me tremble with fear. I gathered myself and sped out of the gate. Unfortunately, I never made it to the gate. Two men closed it and caught me. My hands were tied and they said to the woman that they had been monitoring my movement for a while.

With the rise of terrorist attacks, suicide bombings and kidnappings in Europe, I was in a lot of trouble. They took me into an isolated room. The director and all the important members of the school were present. I became pale as the chief security bombarded me with questions which then was followed by the school director. I cried and pleaded "I am not a terrorist and I have no ill aims. All I wanted was to meet the director because I was told by a member of staff that, he was the only person that could admit me as a student here."

I heard a voice saying "these boys are well trained, he will never tell us what his plans were, let's call the police and they'll take care of him."

My dark pitiful face turned red. I looked at the people in front of me and wished they could give me a chance to one day become like them. I cried not to be taken to the police but they all seemed to be scared of me.

The school director was an excellent psychiatrist and above all a God fearing man. He felt pity for me but left the police to do their job. I was taken in a police car to the police station. They interrogated me like a terrorist. I repeated the same words I had told the school authorities still no one believed what I said. I was kept there for days while the police went interrogating people in the camp about me and all their responses gave me a little bit of credit.

I looked at the four walls of the cell and started singing the song my mother always sang to me. It was clear I needed their presence. This song reminded me of the day my father locked my elder brother and I in our room for a whole day. We were jealous of our sister who always brought good grades from school and had all the favour of our father. We tempered with her report card from school.

When our sister Muma discovered this, she wept endlessly and was inconsolable. We had never seen our father getting angry before. He locked us up in the room for a whole day, for us to battle with our consciences. When we were let out, we came creeping on our knees begging for forgiveness to the whole family. Our father was happy that we were sorry for what we did and reminded us that education is the best weapon we can have to protect us in this world. He was so proud of the enthusiasm his little daughter had for studies. He always sang her praises and always told her "Keep up my precious flower one day you will be the first female to lead this country and all the men will respect and obey you."

Muma was growing up with these dreams in her mind and the whole family was encouraging and cheering her up. Our father used her determination to boost our moral. He encouraged us to work harder and to never be at the mercy of our wives.

Endlessly he told us the story of a lazy man who was at the mercy of his wife. She molested him at will. One day after he had received serious beaten from the wife, he ran and hid himself under the bed and the wife was shouting "come out, come out from there" and with a crying voice he responded "no I will not." Their neighbour always heard them fighting. That day, they came in their numbers to stop him from beating his wife as they thought. When they entered the room, they saw the wife up and fine. They asked "Where is your husband?" with a wounded voice, she responded, "that's him under the bed." They looked at each other and one went closer to the bed and asked him to come out. He said he will not come out. His neighbours insisted and he responded with all the determination on earth, "No! I am a man and I stick to my words, I said I won't come out."

Years later, this story still made me laugh. How come he called himself a man? I asked to myself. The investigation yielded no fruit and the school authorities were call to discharge the case and I was freed.

CHAPTER NINE:
THE NEW CHALLENGE

◆ ◆ ◆

The school director bailed me and told me that I was free. I was happy to be out but my determination be educated had not changed. Instead, the dream of my father made me more eager to go to school. The man was surprise with my determination. I closed my eyes and said "Sir, I have a dream and you are the only one to help me attain it." The director looked at me and asked "How can I help you attain your dreams? By the way what are you dreaming of?" Without any hesitation, I replied "Please sir, help me to go to school. I will work all the cleaning jobs in school to compensate for my fees. I want to have a better future and I need to be educated first. Please help me, sir." The educator grew weak when he heard this. Never someone had pleaded to him to be educated. He thought it wise to know more about me and asked me to come to his office the next day.

"At last!" I said to myself someone believes in me. That night, I sat by a tree beside the school. I did not want to go far and be late for the meeting. I was only thinking about the conversation that I was about to have the next day.

I was awakened by sweet bird's melodies that sang me words of courage and comfort. I stood there till I saw the director's car entering the school. A few minutes later, I followed. I was stopped by the angry gate man who had been sanctioned by the school authorities due to my last infiltrations.

He drove me bitterly and did not want to hear what I was saying. I insisted and the man took it as a challenge. Both of us were determined to attain our objectives. As I persisted, the gate man arrested and pulled me in his small cabin. He called for the school administrator and they all came out as if they were going to war. The woman from the other day came and scowled at me. She said "I knew it! This boy is out for something bad. Go and inform the director while I call the police." I screamed in a fearful voice "please Madame call the director first, he is the one who asked me to come. Don't call the police please."

Before she could take any actions, news came to her from the director instructing her to bring me to his office. She obeyed timidly and wondered what her boss could want from such a "mess" as she referred to me. I was taken to the director and he asked them to be left alone with me. I narrated to him all the tribulation I had gone through from that infamous birthday night until I entered the school and was arrested by the police.

The silent listener sat weakened and heartbroken from the sad story he heard. He did all he could not to shed tears. I was in tears during the narration. He gave me powerful words of comfort and asked me to keep having faith in God. The director asked for me to wait outside while he had a staff meeting with all his personnel. He told them he was intending to give me a change to study and needed their support. Many supported the idea but not all. That mean woman who acts as the vice director led the group of those against. She spoke furiously with her eye glasses on her nose looking at the teachers with intimidation in her eyes. No one looked at her straight in the eyes. She asked "What come if he is aggressive? Who knows what his real intensions are?!"

The director assured them that he would take care of that. He concluded that I should be given a school uniform and all the necessary school supplies. I was like a shy bird when I was given all this. I went to the director and in a slow tune I said "thank you, thank you, sir." The God fearing man tapped me on the shoulder and said "make me proud my boy." I was to live somewhere on the grounds with some personnel.

My first day was more difficult than I had thought. Everyone looked at me in fear. Their eyes told me I was not part of them. As I entered the class, my heart raced and I couldn't stop my legs from trembling. I did not want to be noticed but they were all pointing at me. I greeted timidly and no one answered. I walked to an empty seat at the back of the class and those that were seated around there carried their belongings and transferred to seats far from me.

This was the second worst day in my life. How I wished I could disappear from that spot. I remembered the promise I made to the director and this gave me courage to stand such humiliation. The teacher came in and I was relieved. Perhaps now the focus wouldn't be on me. She called me up and presented me to the pupils and asked them to accept me as a friend. From their reactions I knew this was not to come soon.

Days passed and I took my studies very seriously. Thanks to the awful experiences I faced on the streets back home, I was now equipped to face many challenges. I was mocked and mistreated everyday by the pupils from the older classes. They abused me and sang songs with biting words. They kept tempting my temper with angry words. I gave a deaf ear to all they said. I have been through worse. I looked at them as little babies to whom life had showed its best smiles.

The only worries I had was when the vice director was around. She was always bitter with me and looked at me in terror. My dearest wish was to tell her all what I thought of her but couldn't do such. I kept on feeding the hatred that I bore her. The director was a very busy man. I saw him once in a while but he kept asking my progression to the institutors and was pleased with what he heard.

The next day the others and I were given homework. We were to write about any particular topic at heart. I went back reflecting on what to write. I had many things to say about Africa; war, poverty, education, love and nature. I took my pen that night wrote about war.

"We keep asking ourselves why war is leading in the world today. We want it to end but still we keep on manifesting hatred and wickedness in our daily lives. We forget that the hatred that we manifest individually everyday is what grows up globally and results in war. My dream is to change the world and make it a peaceful place but all I have is a smile. A sincere smile can eliminate the concept of racism and religious differences. A smile brings people closer and this generates love thereby reducing the promoters of war".

With these words, I went to bed and I realised that I could speak better with a pen than through my lips. Each pupil brought his work the next day and the class mistress went through them keenly. She read my work three times successively, and each time she read it, her mind was filled with wonders. She looked at the innocent boy with his shy face and wondered what was going through my mind. She went to her colleagues and presented them the work. They were all astonished at the end. The instructor did not go to the vice director because she knew well how she would react. She kept it to show the director.

CHAPTER TEN:
EXPULSION FROM SCHOOL

◆ ◆ ◆

My image was changing in the minds of the school teachers and this angered some pupils. The Director always took me as an example when counselling the bigger student. This only increased their hatred for me and intensified their oppression. My movements were monitored and they surrounded me at the stairs. "Look at this monkey they say I should take an example from. I have kept these bananas for you". One of them uttered. He threw it at me. "You don't belong to this place and we don't want you here," He concluded. I looked at them and did not offer a word. Before I could realise it, they pushed me down stairs. I tumbled over and over. They warned me "The next time we see you, you'll have yourself to blame, monkey."

I fell badly and was unconscious. Some student passing by found me lying and ran to call for a teacher. I was taken to the hospital. I had many bruises and a broken ankle. I complained that I was attacked by some racist students but couldn't identify their names. The director was furious but knew most of the children had grown up with such a racial hatred from their parents. The man encouraged me and assured me that I was better off than most of them. "Don't let their emptiness and wickedness touch your soul. This world needs boys like you." He concluded.

The Director made a general announcement to the whole school and warned students about racism and violence in school.

That made me look like a rat. I rarely went out of the classroom. Still, letters of hatred with biting words came to me. They wrote letters in which they abused all my family and ancestors. I could not digest these bitter words. I went to their corridor furiously with eyes filled with anger and met some of them. "Say anything you want on me but you never insult my family or my ancestors," I said to them.

One of them got up angrily "so the monkey can talk," he answered. I went on "I pity your ignorance and shame your emptiness. When next you say evil on my ancestors, the monkey in front of you will show you how we do with unripe bananas like you." My words only made them angrier and they jumped on me like wild cats. I engaged into a terrible fight against all of them. Since I was certain to be fighting for a right course, I fought with the extremes of anger and courage. The name of my brave ancestors that I was defending kept circulating in my mind and their strength entered in me.

Teachers alongside the security men came and separated the fight. I was bleeding and the four boys were on the floor seriously bleeding. Those with broken noses cried, calling for their parents. Everyone was shocked to see such a horrible scene. The director ordered that they should be taken to the hospital. The parents of the other boys were informed. They were not happy. The families ordered for my immediate dismissal or they would take the school to court. The director called for an emergency meeting with the parents of the school. The parents formed a coalition supported by the vice director who had got a perfect motive to expel me from the school.

The meeting was convened at 9:00 am and every one came tensed and nervous. I sat in a nearby class, listening to all that was said. I knew I had put the director in a difficult position and was ashamed of myself. But internally, I did not regret what I did.

In the hall, the parents barked at the director and said what they had asked for was final. The director gave all the excuses and reasoning he could but the parents seemed well fortified against any words he said. He went out and brought me in the hall. Most of the parents seemed to be born from the same racist womb, as they looked at me bitterly. The director called for their inner most consciences. He asked them to have pity on me "look at him, all he demands is to be educated and change the world. Give him that opportunity and together lets change the world and make it a better place."

These words forced tears out of my eyes. Some parents were affected but not all. I begged them with many tears but their determination had transformed their heart to a stone. The director sat weak on his chair. I turned to him and in a slow voice I said "Sir, I know I have failed my promises I gave you, but sir they insulted my origins and my ancestors. I couldn't allow them because their memories are the only thing I have in this world. Nelson Mandela, Nkwame Nkrumah, Um Nyobe, Mohammed Kaddafi, Thomas Sankara; I am proud of them and will defend their names everywhere I go. Thank you sir for your humanity and generosity, I hope you'll forgive me."

The director couldn't resist these powerful confessions and burst into tears in front of the parents. My heart stopped beating as I saw my mentor crying. Some parents sat there silent, feeling guilty to have destroyed a dream and thus a generation. I ran out of the hall and went out of the gate running in tears in an unknown direction.

CHAPTER ELEVEN:
DANY IS REUNITED WITH HIS FAMILY

◆ ◆ ◆

Meanwhile, back in the streets in my country, life was gradually gaining momentum since the war had ended for more than a year now. The rebels had surrendered and civilians had regained the street. Each went on recounting the effects of the war on them and their families. People still felt the stigma of the war.

My mother for close to a year had been working as a maid in a wealthy home. Since she was released, she had nowhere to go and no food to eat. She had no choice than to support all the demands imposed on her by her hosts. The other maids were always consoling her since she was always in tears. At night when her patrons were relaxing, she always went out secretly and patrolled the streets with the aim of seeing me or my sister Muma. She was doing this for close to a year now to no avail.

Every night when she came back, tears of sorrows ran all through her eyes. One maids called Boyin who was close to her, asked her "But why all these tears and sorrows?" My mother started recounting from that famous night "My husband and my first son were shot in front of me. My daughter and I were bundled and carried away. My little boy was left alone in the house with two corpses. My daughter was carried to another rebel's camp and only God knows what they did to her. Now where are my boy and my daughter? Tell me what else can I do than shed these tears for them?"

The other maids were sulky as they listened. They did all they could to prevent their eyes from been wet but the stubborn tears forced their way out and the whole room almost became swampy. Powerful words of comfort came out of their mouths. Each of them concluded saying God is still alive.

The lady of the house was a fashionista with a difficult character. She had no mastery of how to control children and the only reason she kept my mother was because she needed her help and expertise. On several occasions she repeated these disheartening words "If not for these children I would have sent you out of this house." My mother gave a deaf ear to what she said. The only maid that went close to the fashionista was Cinta, who had gained her favor because she was her reporter and great gossip. To the other maids, she wasn't a friend. My mother patiently waited for night to go on her mission.

Far down south, girl who had been captured had formed a coalition there. Their new life was in line with what they went through in the rebel's camp. The rebels had destroyed their dreams of living a decent life. High wave of prostitution, binge drinking and drugs were in their order of daily life.

Muma, my sister was one of them. Since the day they had separated her from my mother, she had been traumatized by the experience. Their release and exposure had made them live at the mercy of others. Muma and her friends were prey to hungry wolves in the streets. The girls became heartless and fearless, ready to do anything to survive.

Muma had never forgotten her family. She sometimes sat at one corner crying and regretting what she had become. She had several times thought of committing suicide "After all who is going to regret a disaster like me?" she said to herself. She thought of the virtues of a good woman that our mother used to inculcate her and with no regret she said "Life and men had decided otherwise".

Back overseas I was growing pale day by day. The comeback of terrorist attack in overseas countries intensified the level of police controls in the streets. Added to this, the insecurity in the Middle East had increased the number of oversea seekers and all of them came to look for a better future. I started missing my country and the few peaceful weeks I had had with Uncle Sam. A recent ship wreck had plunge the whole camp in to desolation as those who had lost family members were inconsolable. I became certain that nothing in life was worth giving up your family and no happiness could be enjoyed without the family.

I thought of how to reunite with my family in my own way. I first thought of arranging mud statues but realized this was impossible since mud could not be seen easily. I looked around me and saw a stone. Immediately I thought of carving the names of my family on five large rocks where I could sit in between, but where was I to find such rocks.

I sat hopeless and helpless. The gentle wind blew in the trees around and it seemed their leaves were talking to me. I looked up the tree and a joyful smile appeared on his face. I remembered the love my father had for trees and decided to make it my new family. With a knife, I carved the names of my family members on the trees around myself. I gave each tree a name but the distance between the trees did not suit me. I wanted to bring them closer as a family. Since the only way was to plant new ones, I went around looking for seeds.

I looked for five seeds which I planted and carved the names of my family members on. Added to me alive we were six and reunited. I planted them in a circular form as a family dining on the same table. I spent most of my time in the middle of these trees. For the one bearing my father's name, I talked to it as if I was talking to my father with all the due respect. Every time I was to eat, I watered the trees as to permit them to eat also. I recounted stories on events that had once made us laughed. These memories made me happy as smiles were visible all over my face and in a slow tune I said "Thank you Lord." To me the Almighty had shown me the way. I started looking for materials and trees to reunite my family in many places.

Outside of the camp I carried my projects wherever I could; five trees were planted because the sixth person was still alive. I gave them names and took special care of them. As I sat conversing with the trees, the passersby stopped and observed me closely. Others took photos of me and I paid little concern to them. I sat by the side of my trees looking tired and confessed to my parents "the world is full of evil. It is very hard for a righteous person to be happy. Everywhere, evil people keep tempting me with temptation. Father I'm scared of one day becoming like them."

CHAPTER TWELVE:
THE COURAGE OF A MOTHER

◆ ◆ ◆

I had launched a green revolution without knowing. My trees were spreading everywhere. I had become a geek and people were impressed by the passion and energy I put in it. The names carried on the trees all over raised people's interest to know their significance. I moved over long distances transporting water to nourish MY family. My alone time with the trees was impressive to all.

Back in my country, my mother had searched in vain for us and almost gave up. She heard over the radio of the stream of abandoned girls down South. She started having strong sentiments about her daughter. These thoughts kept disturbing her and she abandoned her job and started her journey down South. Her friend, Boyin, wasn't so sure as she wondered what would happen to her if her intuition were not correct. She asked "Where will you stay? What will you do? And what about your feeding? Please my friend, don't face the streets." My mother knew her friend was only worried about her wellbeing but her motherly heart had taken a decision and that was final.

That same night she went to her employer to ask for permission to go and search for her child. Immediately as her employer heard this, she twisted her face and this stained her yellow limbs dark. Furiously she burst out "If you step your legs out of this house never you come back here."

My mother knew that drastic times called for drastic measures, she went in her room and gathered what was left of her belongings said her prayers and headed down South. Boyin gathered the little money she had saved and pressed it in her hands. In tears they said good bye to each other.

Down South, Muma and her friends had been overtaken by risky situations and most of them were suffering from chronic infections. They had indulged in too much excesses and this had destroyed their immune systems. Muma had used all the money she had on drugs which could ease the pain temporarily. Her only chance of survival was through an operation. She was admitted in the hospital for some days but later driven out for being unable to pay the bills. She went back to the streets but had no energy to get back to work. Day and night she fought against the pain with no money to buy drugs.

Our mother had reached the South and did not know where to start the search. She went to orphanage, camps and hospitals, she moved about questioning people along the streets. The aged woman was exhausted by the endless walk. She sat to rest on a public seat and was taken away by sleep. She got up in the night and started questioning some street girls around. Some of them under the control of drugs rudely accosted her. Some responded but had no idea of the person she was looking for. As she was going she turned and looked at those innocent girls devastated by life "Oh Father, they are just victims of this wicked world, please protect them" she murmured to herself.

She was directed to a place which served as their "quarter general" by a street girl. The first girl she questioned was in the range 15 to 18. Her eyes looked sleepy. Her eye lids were painted blue and decorated in a special way. Her lips were in a reddish aggressive form. Her mouth was chewing endlessly and the dresses she wore were not of her size. The girl looked at her horizontally and asked "who are you and why are you looking for her?" My almost happy mother replied "I'm her mother. Please tell me where I can find her." The girl directed her the room where Muma was shaking in agony.

The room was like a small cabin over an abandon garage. Even the air in it was contaminated. My mother opened the door and resisted the odour that came out of it. "Muma, Muma my little girl" she said and fell on the bed side and held her in her hands embracing her endlessly. When Muma realized truly it was her mother she skipped out of the bed and gave a cry like that of a new born baby. Continuously she cried "Mummy, mummy, see what they have turned me into, hold me tight mama, don't leave me alone" her mother's heart almost stopped beating.

She cried, begging her child to be strong for her and said "All those who encouraged and promoted this war will answer to God. What is left of this country? Look at those hopeless children outside, where are their parents. Oh men you are wicked." Muma held tight herself to her mother's arm. She was afraid and ashamed of what she had become and did not want to look her straight in her eyes. "Mother, I'm sick, the doctor said I must be operated on, and this requires a huge amount of money. What these men did to me was evil but mother they haven't touched my spirit. I'm still the little girl you cherished years ago."

Our mother was happy and sad at the same time. She gave hope and comfort to her daughter, but did not know where the money for the operation would come from.

Early the next morning she took her daughter back to the North to find safety for her. She went to her maid friends and when they heard the sum needed, they were shocked. They gave her what they had but it couldn't even afford a surgery knife. She sat at the gate waiting for her former boss. The lady arrived and refused to attend to her. After several hours waiting outside, the Madam came out with wickedness showing all over her face and bitterly asked what she wanted. "Please, I need some money for my daughter's operation, and then I will work without any salary for as long as you wish" cried my mother. "Please get out of here. This is not a bank or an orphanage. I have no penny for you and I don't need your services anymore. Move out of here, nonsense." The fashionista retorted and ordered the gate to be closed.

My mother took my sister and they left. There was no need to wait for the man of the house because he did everything the wife wanted. The other maids hanging at one end of the gate were devastated when they heard the response of their boss. "Hash, certainly being rich is equal to being heartless. They preferred seeing their dog well fed than saving an innocent soul. Where is mankind going to?" cried Boyin.

CHAPTER THIRTEEN:
DANY IS OFFERED A JOB

◆ ◆ ◆

The two unfortunate women were moving to an unknown direction, Muma turned toward my mother and said "Mother I can't bear seeing you suffer this way for me. You know well no one can help us and I know I'm going to pass away. Please mother…….." She was stopped by her mother who knew what she wanted to say. She kept on giving her hope and concluded "God is still alive."

All the hardship Muma had gone through and was still going through made her see things the way life demanded and not by the way God wanted. "Mother I'm not sure he is still alive. If truly he is, he dwells only with the rich. How can he allow all these things to happen to me," asked Muma. Her mother was scared hearing her speak like that. She rather understood how aggravated her child was. She told her never to respond to evil by evil because this will give evil more credit. She also warned her never to doubt God's actions because He will give the evils a taste of their own medicine." It was clear Muma was looking for every means to make someone pay for her ill-luck. If she could contaminate the whole world then her mind would be in peace. Lucky enough her mother found her in time before she could awake the monster sleeping inside of her.

Overseas, I continued uniting my family. I had planted a considerable number of trees alone that left nobody indifferent. I was happy to see my trees growing well. I sat with my family looking at my father and asked, "daddy are we witnessing the end of the world? Nature is becoming hostile and mankind also is becoming hostile. Terrorist cause sorrows to humanity in the name of religion. How can people join and support such a course?"

How I wished my father could answer me. A voice retorted from behind "Hello boy." I did not know someone was behind him. I jumped up rapidly looking at the trees round me. I thought my hallucination was real. I looked keenly to see which tree had spoken to me. The voice came again. "Hello boy, are you okay?" I turned and came back to my senses. I saw a man standing behind me. Without giving any response I took my bucket and started running as fast as I could. The man shouted at me to wait but I had gone far. I thought they had come to arrest me since other men were seated inside a car parked by the road side.

The man in question was Mr. Turner. He was a member of a Non Governmental Organization (NGO) on climate change. He saw the same names on the trees as those he has seen on the others and was more eager to speak to me. The whole day I did not show myself. I came and watered the younger plants only at night. I knew arresting me would bury my happiness.

Mr. Turner searched for me in all the sites I planted my trees. He posted his men in almost all the sites but I did not show up. I was invisible for some days and was already missing my family. I made my way to one of the sites. Looking left and right, the man posted at the other end immediately knew I was the one. He alerted Mr. Turner who drove to the site without hesitating. The men stood at a distance watching at me so as not to scare me.

I was explaining to my family my absence. Suddenly, I heard a voice behind me. I turned and realized he was standing right there. I saw the man with the imposing body right behind him. His face looked fierce and friendly, certainly because he was smiling. His clothing was neat and fit him well. By his side were two men and a woman almost of sandwich generation.

My eyes were filled with wonders as I concentrated on her. Her eyes were gentle as the rising moon. From her lips even mountain and ocean would obey. Her body was like that of a one month baby "certainly she must be a fee" I said to myself.

"How come I'm still here waiting for my arrest? This beautiful monster has certainly done something bad to me," silently I thought, before I burst out asking what misdemeanor had I committed. Mr. Turner peacefully responded "nothing boy, absolutely nothing. We are not here to arrest you but to talk with you. Please don't run away." I was confused as to how come people had taken interest in me.

I was however not convinced and asked, "talk about what? If I may ask." Mr Turner came closer to me. My heart started racing "Are you the one who planted all these trees?' The man asked. "Yes" I replied, "but I was trying to reunite my family. I didn't mean to…. "!! "No, no, is ok" the man said. He had noticed the fear in me.

Mr. Turner proposed that we should sit down and do presentation and explain why they are after me. I accepted but kept my eyes far from the girl with them. I knew looking at her eyes could make you accept white as being black. The man sat next to me and went, on "I'm Mr. Turner and these are my colleagues; Mr. Watford, Mr. Donavan and Miss Marylyn. "The fee also has a name but what if she was real? No, never…

how come she immobilized my legs with her eyes. I was speaking to myself when I heard the presentation.

"We are members of an N.G.O on Environment and Climate Change. We carry out environmental campaigns and its effects on climate change. Studies have proved that the world is becoming hotter every year, and in not more than a century, the inhabitants of the world will all perish from the heat."

I was looking at them almost confused. I wondered why all this grammar on saving the world. I began doubting if they saw me as a super hero. And even if I could, what good has the world done to me. I was impatient to go back to my me time.

"We, in the same way as the United Nations (U.N.) promote and encourage people to plant trees and embark on a green revolution to cool the world and protect future generations. We have seen the wonderful job you have done so far and how you humanize the trees. I wanted to know what your motivation is and if you can motivate others if necessary and why not the whole world" he said.

CHAPTER FOURTEEN:
THE CLIMATE CHANGE AMBASSADOR

◆ ◆ ◆

My fears transformed to courage. My hopelessness began tilting towards hope. I was still ignorant of what life had in store for me. I told them about the war events in my country. The insecurity that reigned, up to that pathetic night. My mysterious survival to a ship wreck. How I decided to reunite my family through planting of trees. Mr. Turner and his colleagues were speechless. This was the most sorrowful and moving story they had ever heard. He looked at me as I was in tears and said "Come, we are going to take care of you.'

Marylyn was in a traumatize state. She put on her sunglasses in order not to show that she was in tears. As they were going, I heard a soft voice with a charming tune saying to me "Your family, where ever they are, will be proud of your courage." These words penetrated me and struck my heart with euphoria. I murmured "Maybe with her magic she can tell me where my mother and sister are. Then I will be her loyal servant. But how can I ask her this little favour?"

Mr. Turner took me to their head office. After lunch, he narrated the same story I had told them. The hall was silent. They were all carried away by the melancholy that they all sat still as mounted figures. The silent listeners were carried away by the sadness of the story and couldn't imagine the new ideas to work on for their green revolution campaigns. Mr. Turner muttered, "Hmm planting trees in memory of your family or immortalizing the love and unity of your family by planting trees for each member of your family , both living or death. So that you might live together forever." The sadness on people's faces dissipated. The dramatic postures in which they were sitting addressed to an upright postures. Together they joined their hands to applaud their new campaign strategy. Everyone came to congratulate me. They pressed my hands and gave me a smile of comfort and courage. I still did not realize what was happening. To me, it was just a dream as I used to have. How come, all of a sudden I was to become the savior of the world?

I was expecting it to end soon and I going back to my habitual life. Instantly, I was given a shelter while they were putting things together. For the first time in forever, I had a descent shower and a night as in my la-la land. The tender and soft bed prolonged my awakening hours. Mr. Turner woke me up and as soon as I took my breakfast, we left for the office. "Lord, I beg of you, may this dream never end and if this is reality may your name be praised," I said to God.

We entered the office and everyone welcomed me with due respect. My eyes caught those of Marylyn and I threw them elsewhere. She came to us, greeted Mr. Turner then turned to me. I stared at her and my innocent eyes almost fell off. She smiled at me and I felt my soul leaving my body. Mr. Turner left to attend to other people. My heart urged me to ask what I had been thinking the day before, but my mouth refused to be the one to do so. She came closer to me and said she was sorry for the tragedy I had gone through. I was confused. I looked at her and asked "Are you real" Marylyn looked at me surprised "What do you mean if I am real?" she asked. I was trembling. My senses were uncontrollable. Timidly I asked "Are you not the queen of the fees?' Marylyn was confused. She now understood why I had been silent whenever she was around. She went on "Do I look like a fee?' I replied "the last time I saw a similar beauty to yours was in a fee movie. We were told that fees were the most beautiful creatures that existed."

The girl burst into laughter. Her voice was softer and more tender than a caress. Her half closed eyes were like a shy rainbow. Like an orchid, her beauty illuminated the hall. My dark face almost turned red and my enamored heart almost quarreled with my mouth, to help express its wish. Marylyn said "I am just a human as you and anyone else in this office. Fees exist only in our imaginations." Instantly I replied "If what you are saying is true then the god of beauty has been unjust to other people."

Marylyn was twice as old as I. Her beauty made her win the favors of everyone she met. She seldom took interest in people's life but my story had impressed her. Mr. Turner came in with good news. My story was to be rewritten and published by a famous publishing house and sold worldwide. Added to that, it was a new dawn for the new campaign strategy.

I was taken to the campaign grounds. The media and press rallied to see the new brain behind the fight against climate change. They had come to hear me talk to them and to the world at large. Mr. Turner did not think I was capable of speaking directly to the world but I had gone through tougher situations than that.

I accepted and stood right in front of the camera "my name is Tem Dany, I lost my family on my seventh birthday and I had to face life alone in a country plagued by war. I left to pursue happiness overseas that is what took me to this country. I began planting trees ignorantly to reunite my family till I was told that these trees could act against climate change and save the world and future generation. Now, I have a more important reason than just reuniting my family. Our leaders are putting in theirs, with all the conventions they are signing. Let everyone plant a tree for each member of their family as a way of immortalizing their family and save the planet. Then we can stand before the Almighty with a clear conscience of having done our part to protect the world and humanity. Thanks."

People did not want me to stop talking. They sat static and perplexed at my speech. After my last words, I had to stand again for some seconds before the crowd could get back to their normal mode. Unanimously, they put their hands together and applauded my bravery and intelligence. I became the world ambassador on climate change.

CHAPTER FIFTEEN:
DANY BRINGS SMILES TO REFUGEE CAMPS

◆ ◆ ◆

My speech was retransmitted by several media stations and also debated by important personalities. My pictures were posted in the streets and at campaign rallies. I became an icon. My book went across boundaries and all who read each had their own lessons and personal impressions. All over the world people began planting trees in memory of their lost ones. Others were rekindling the love and unity of their living family. Never in the history of mankind had an environmental campaign been so successful. I was invited to international conferences and during my talks I reminded world leaders of the inverse relationship between education and terrorism. I told them "promoting youth education will reduce their involvement in acts of terrorism." I encourage the African youth to believe in the power of a dream and to never give in to hopelessness.

Meanwhile, my mother and sister had found refuge in a home of the homeless. My sister was dying and my mother was helpless. Every morning my mother went to a waste discharge to search for metals and bottles to sell. She used the money to buy drugs and food. Boyin collected food remains and secretly took it to them to combat hunger.

One day my mother on her way back from the waste discharge saw a huge poster on a sign board on the street. From a distance she saw the boy on it resembled her son. She was not certain but went closer to the sign board. She noticed it was me, her son standing there smiling and looking at her. Her dull face became bright and smiles were visible all over her face. Her heart was submerged with joy and in a tired voice, she asked "My son is that you? Where are you and why is your picture posted here?"

Since she could not read what was written on the poster, she thought of the worst. "Oh my god no, not my son, what will I become without my children. Please Father, not my Dany," she exclaimed. She was convinced the posters hung on the streets were for people found dead somewhere. She immediately burst into tears and went where my sister was.

She told her why she was crying and they both became inconsolable.

Muma started calling for death in a loud voice and this only increased her pains. A few minutes later, Muma started rolling on the floor. The pains became unbearable, her confused mother held her on her knees touching her all over her body. In our mother tongue she pleaded with Muma not to abandon her in this dangerous world. Muma fell asleep on my mother's knees. My mother kept watching her all night in case she needed her. The whole night she sang sorrowful choruses for her son and her daughter's lives.

Early the next morning, her friend who was heading to the market passed by to give them some food. She explained how life had pierced her once more. She took her friend to the poster and said "that is my son Dany, death has taken him away." Boyin read all what has been written on the poster and asked "But who told you he was dead? If truly this is your son, then he is an important personality from what is written there."

My mother couldn't believe what she heard. There was a total pandemonium in her brain. "What are you saying? It means he is not dead?" she asked. Being alive was all what she wanted to know. She could not imagine any possibility of me becoming a VIP. Boyin was surprised at her reactions and said

"My friend it seems you did not hear what I said. This boy here is an environment ambassador. He should be very rich; he can put an end to your sufferings." My mother was almost in tears, she replied, "My son is alive. Did they write where we can find him?" Boyin realized how motherly she was. Even in the worst form of misery and poverty, she preferred to hear that her son is alive rather than that he is rich. She went back to inform her daughter of the news.

I had no time for myself again. I either had to attend intensive classes and seminars or sign dedications for my book. I was living in a luxurious mansion. Within this short while, I had accumulated wealth that even in my craziest dreams I couldn't have thought of. I had people who took care of my clothing, food, and health. Mr. Turner and Marylyn were my closest advisers.

I sat alone in my room and asked myself if truly I was happy despite all I had. I thought of my family and old Sam. I realized money is nothing if you are not with the people that matter in your life. I now understood what my father meant when he said "Nothing in life is worth without the family." I needed to do something to feel happy. I organized with Mr. Turner and others to help refugees.

We went to the camp with some basic necessities and distributed to all. I went to them and gave them hope and courage. I convinced N.G.O's and volunteers to put in more finance into assisting refugees. I pleaded with my friends to help me search for my family. They agreed to organize a trip to my country.

CHAPTER SIXTEEN:
THE NATIONAL HERO

◆ ◆ ◆

My partners and I arrived in my country, both for the environmental campaign and to search for my family. The authorities had not yet restored total control of the towns. We were however welcomed by some authorities. I was received as a national hero. Together with the authorities we discussed the importance of a forestation and its impact on the climate.

We went to schools and encouraged pupils to join us and save the world. I was overtaken by hurt and disappointment. The youth in my country did not believe in anything any longer. Life to them was like a vampire film which they themselves were acting. I was in the mist of people as an important figure. My memories were pushing me far behind my childhood and the trauma I had lived. Finding my family was the only thing that mattered to me. I was taken to the radio station and I made the announcement over the radio. Everywhere I went people ran to me as if I was a Messiah. However, I felt bad each time because they needed not only words of comfort but a helping hand.

I decide to trace my childhood. I started by visiting the house of my father. When we got closer, my legs tightened on the ground and I began moving slowly. Everyone understood I was not ok. My head went down and my eyes were in tears. Mr. Turner patted me on my shoulders as to ask me to be strong. We saw what was remaining of the house. I went to where my father was buried and fell on my knees. "Father, I am back, I realize all the dreams you had for this house. Just help me find mother and Muma. Thank you father for all you did to me, forever you shall be my hero. Rest in Peace."

We equally visited all the camps that had harbored me in the past. There, I recognized many people I left behind and I brought joy to the whole camp. Those to whom I stole money, I refunded them with a considerable sum. I equally went to all the places I slept and the hospitals that treated me.

I entered the park where Old Sam was working. Sam was in his room resting and I asked my crew to wait, I went and knocked Uncle Sam's house which had also been mine. The old man aggressively opens the door because no one ever came there to look for him. His eyes grew bigger when he saw me. He threw himself on me and took me in. "It's you my boy, tell me how life has treated you there. You look very clean and these clothes you are wearing, to whom they belong?" The old man asked. I replied "Uncle Sam they are mine. I'm a rich man now and you are too from today on." The old man looked at me perplexed and speechless. He went down on his knees and tears ran down his cheeks for the first time "so God has remembered me indeed, oh thank you Lord." I held him up and took him out. I presented him to my new friend's and they were all happy to see him.

Uncle Sam was surprised at how these people knew about him. He was told that the whole world knew him because he is an important personality in my book. Uncle Sam brought laughter at the park as he boasted proudly skipping from one end to the other, saying to the other worker in the park that he is a hero. He went all round the park shouting "Who wants to touch the hero, don't be ashamed, the hero is here." Old Sam was taken in and given special care.

I was worried since the radio announcement did not bear any fruit in my search for my family. I went to many radio stations and asked them to insist and repeatedly sing the story on the radio. There was no way my family could hear the announcement since only rich people listened to the radio.

The friend of my mother was busy cleaning the plates and singing, when the news was airing and her attention was drowned only when she heard the name of Muma, she ran by the door but it was over. Her heart was beating endlessly and her worries were seen all over her face. She began turning around the parlor because her employer was seated inside. The information began again and when she heard it, the glass she was holding fell from her hand and she shouted the name of my mother then closed her mouth with her hand. Her employer dashed to the scene and started rebuking her and informed her that her salary will suffer the consequences.

Boyin did not respond. After picking the broken glass, she ran into her room and changed her dresses before she could step her legs in the parlor to ask for permission, her boss said she was going nowhere. She ordered her to go back to her room and resume duty. "I don't care who is looking for her or how she is, you are going nowhere," said the fashionista. The maid could not digest these bitter words from her boss. She retorted "You are a witch with a stone at the place of a heart. You call yourself a mother?! Let me tell you, you are a shame to humanity because you don't deserve to be called a mother. For my salary you can keep it and may it fill your empty life."

With these words she went and the whole house was as silent as an empty stadium. Her employer speechlessly watched her going out. She was bubbling with anger. Her bright face turned dark as she took the way to her room. The other maids looked at each other and were happy their friend had hit the nail on the head. They ran to their head quarters feeling proud and released. The heroin departed directly to where her friend was camping.

CHAPTER SEVENTEEN: THE TELEVISION PROGRAM

♦ ♦ ♦

A TV program was organized where we were to encourage people on tree planting. My mother was informed about the program by her friend and that I was in the country and was searching for them. Her heart raced as she heard this. "Where is he? Please take me to him," she said smiling. Muma was still lying on the floor very weak, she heard all they said and insisted on going with them. She said "Let me see my little sibling before I die. I need to talk to him for the last time." Boyin took her on her back and they went to a radio station in town and they presented themselves. Immediately Mr. Turner was phoned by the people of the radio and given the news.

They were still at the plateau and Mr. Turner eclipsed himself and sent two of his collaborators to go get them at the radio station. He wanted to surprise me, so he did not tell me anything. The two men brought the three women at the national television premises and they were kept in a waiting room. Mr. Turner received confirmation that they had arrived. After we had answered all the questions posed by the journalist, Mr. Turner himself took his turn "Permit me use this opportunity to thank someone who has given a soul to our project. If we succeed in this mission then humanity will always remember that it was a courageous soul that took the lead. I'm honored to be a living testimony of this young boy whose life has been governed by the audacity of hope and bravery. My boy, The Almighty has heard your cry."

Everyone on the platform was surprised and wondered where he was heading with this. I was even more confused because Mr. Turner had never been that serious when referring to me. Mr. Turner then requested, "Bring them in." Immediately three shabby looking women dressed with poverty all over them came in. Their hair was scattered and dirty. Their shoes dilapidate. Everyone on the platform was muddled.

I recognized the woman that had nursed me all my childhood and protected me against any malice. I did not care if the whole world was looking at me. She is my mother. In a thunderous voice I rumbled, "Mamaaaaaaaaaaaaaaa!." I jumped from my seat and ran towards them. The cameramen focused their cameras to capture all the powerful images portrayed. My mother responded to my cry and also shouted running her tired legs towards me." Danyy...y.., Danyy...y" and I skipped in her arms crying, "Mama...Ma". Muma joined us shouting my name "Dany, my Dany." No one in the platform could restain their tears. Boyin cried for all the pain her friend had gone through.

I held my mother so tight and screamed her name continuously. My mother understood that my shouting was a means for me to recount to her all the sufferings I had gone through. All parents understand such screams from their children and she condoned to my melancholy only through tears. Mr. Turner himself was on tears with all the journalists present. Even the viewers watching the program at home were touched by the moving images. Tears of joy ran in various homes. Most parents held their families tight to them to feel the joy of being together in peace.

The organizer of the program was in such emotions that he held the microphone for some minutes looking at the brave woman in tears holding her children. Everyone looked at me, who a few minutes ago looked solid as a rock, now I was so weak and feeble as a frightened child. The journalist in a soft tune said "The love between a mother and her children is like a burning fire with no amount of water capable of putting it out. Mother is a person who was not created on fear but on courage and determination." Thanks to all mothers of the world.

Muma's weak body could not resist all the emotions in the hall. She fell right in front of the camera and went into a coma. There was total panic in the studio. The program was interrupted and my mother and I became confused and inconsolable. Mr. Turner and the others hurriedly rushed her to the hospital while Marylyn and my family members followed from behind.

CHAPTER EIGHTEEN:
THE HAPPY FAMILY

◆ ◆ ◆

Who would have thought that a TV campaign program could turn into an event that caught the reaction of viewers all over the world? The highest personalities in my country endlessly called to know the health status of Muma? Doctors were dispatched from all over to put their experience together to keep her alive. The charges for her operation were taken care of by the state. Muma was out of danger and we paid her a visit with my mother's friend. I narrated to them how I got to my success. My mother kept thanking God for all He had done. I presented Uncle Sam to my family and they were all glad to see him.

My family and I received an invitation from the president. We were to dine with our interim president. During the dinner, we discussed the impact created by their program to unite families separated by war in our countries and worldwide. The President declared the intension of the government to unite families separated by war in our country.

Muma also insisted on rehabilitating the vulnerable girls who had embraced prostitution as the only way to survive. The reaction was immediate as prostitutes were sheltered, fed and encouraged to live a decent life and engaged in decent economic activities. Muma became a newbie on a national group promoting education of young girls. They pointed out and explained all the vices faced by uneducated girls. My mother took her friend Boyin everywhere we went. The house of my late father was re-built and up graded. I took my family and friend's overseas to show them the legacy I had planted there.

Henceforth they had everything they had dreamt of. Despite all the wealth, my mother maintained her modesty and simplicity. We devoted our lives and wealth to those that needed support. I found happiness looking at all the people smiling around me. I was glad to have fulfilled not only my dreams but those of my father. For what it is worth, I had pursued my happiness and would live it till the end.

www.ingramcontent.com/pod-product-compliance
Lightning Source LLC
Chambersburg PA
CBHW022044170626
46808CB00003B/1361